A Hen FOR Izzy Pippik

WRITTEN BY Aubrey Davis

ILLUSTRATED BY Marie Lafrance

Kids Can Press

Shaina perched on the porch with her eyes shut and listened. Mama's sewing machine chattered in the kitchen. Baby Pinkus pounded a pot. Grandpa whistled an old-time tune.

In the market across the road, a nanny goat bleated. A truck puttered past. A cuckoo cooed from Mr. Fine's clock shop.

Shaina wished she could still dust for Mr. Fine. She wished she could help the other merchants, too. But people had little to spend these days. There were few shoppers in the market and fewer jobs to do. Times were tough.

Suddenly Shaina felt a pickety peck on her toe. She jumped up and her eyes popped open.

BEE YAAK!

"It's a chicken!" she gasped.

Shaina had never seen such a magnificent hen. She had emerald green feathers with golden speckles, and a ruby red comb.

"Where did you come from? Are you lost?"

Baawwk!

Shaina picked her up and smoothed her feathers.

"Don't worry, little chicken. I'll find out where you live."

The hen snuggled in her arms as Shaina raced across the road to the market. She showed the hen to every shopkeeper and peddler. But nobody had ever seen the beautiful bird before.

"I wish you could tell me where you belong," sighed Shaina.

Buck. Buck. Buck.

Suddenly she spotted two muddy tracks in the road. She followed them to a pothole. Beside it sat a broken wooden crate with a sign that read:

IZZY PIPPIK: CHICKENS AND EGGS.

Shaina grabbed the crate and raced home with the hen squawking behind her.

Mama gasped. Pinkus gurgled. Grandpa smacked his lips.

"Chicken soup?" he asked.

"Fricassee," replied Mama.

"We can't eat her!" Shaina cried. "She belongs to Izzy Pippik."

"Who's he?" Mama asked.

Shaina pointed to his name on the crate. "It's his crate, so it's his chicken. I think she escaped when it fell off his truck."

The hen fluttered onto her shoulder.

"Mama, can I keep her until Izzy Pippik returns?"

"Who says he's coming back, Shaina?"

"He has to, Mama. She's so beautiful."

Winking at Shaina, Grandpa took Mama's hand. "What's it going to hurt?" he asked.

Mama sighed. "For a few days, maybe."

Grandpa helped Shaina make a nest from the crate.
She carefully set the hen inside.
"I'll call you 'Yevka'," she said.
Grandpa grinned. "That's a pretty name, Shainala."

Early the next morning, Yevka cackled loudly. The sleepy family shuffled to the nest where a pearly egg glowed in the straw.

"Scrambled?" asked Grandpa.

"Poached," replied Mama.

Baby Pinkus burped.

"We can't eat this egg!" Shaina frowned.

"Why not?" Mama asked.

"If it's Izzy Pippik's hen, it's his egg, too."

"Eggs don't keep forever," muttered Grandpa.

Shaina laughed. "Mr. Pippik will come before then!"

In a few weeks, twelve fuzzy chicks were peeping and pecking and poking about. They ate the baby's biscuits and spilled Grandpa's soup. They scratched Mama's stockings to pieces. They grew peskier by the day, and Mama's grumbles grew with them.

"Shaina," whispered Grandpa. "Mr. Pippik had better hurry."

"He won't be long, Grandpa."

One morning, two young roosters began to squabble and the whole flock joined in. Teacups crashed. Saucers smashed. Feathers filled the air.

Mama stormed to the cupboard and snatched a broom. "This is not a henhouse!" she hollered. "These birds have got to go!"

"Please, Mama!" Shaina begged. "Let them stay!"

But Mama was in a foul mood. She raised her broom and charged. Squawking chickens flew out the door and onto the road.

The street sweeper gasped. The postman laughed. The beggar smacked his lips.

"Boiled?" he asked.

"Baked," replied the postman.

"Catch them!" the sweeper cried.

With hoots and hollers, the townsfolk poured into the market. They chased the birds under pushcarts, over crates and all around the square.

"Leave them alone!" shouted Shaina. "You can't eat these chickens!"
With hot, hungry eyes, the people swarmed around.
"Why not?" they howled.
Shaina explained that they belonged to Izzy Pippik.
"You silly girl!" they sneered. "He's not coming back!"
"Yes, he will!" Shaina snapped.

Grandpa pushed through the crowd and held her tight.

"This is how you treat an honest little girl?" he thundered. "It'll hurt to wait and see?"

The people blushed and lowered their eyes. One by one, they shuffled away.

"For now, the birds are safe," Grandpa murmured. "But your Izzy Pippik had better come soon."

Shaina kissed his cheek. "He will, Grandpa."

But Izzy Pippik didn't come. As the months passed, Yevka's chicks grew and had chicks of their own. Then they grew up and had chicks, too.

Before long, roosters crowed from rooftops and hens nested in every nook. Hundreds of chickens flapped about the square. They toppled trashcans, fought for food and cackled from morning to night.

They grew rowdier by the day, and the people's grumbles grew with them.

"You're a hard-headed nuisance, Shaina," they hissed. "Your Pippik will never come."

"Yes, he will!" she shouted.

Still he didn't come, though other people did. By foot and by car, they trekked into town. Soon curious sightseers rolled in by the busload to see the great flock. And each night they left with shopping bags bursting with socks, dishes, bagels and more. Every shop in town was open and every shelf was full.

With business booming, people forgot their anger. And Shaina found plenty of jobs again.

One day she was spreading ice for the fishmonger.

"Your chickens make us so happy," he said.

"They're not mine," snapped Shaina. "They belong to Izzy Pippik, so they'll all have to go."

"You're always saying that!" wailed the fishmonger. "Can't you see that they belong here?"

A curious crowd gathered. They moaned and muttered
and started to chant:
WE LOVE THEM!
WE NEED THEM!
WE WANT THEM TO STAY!
Over the hubbub a truck horn blared.

AoooGAH!

"Move aside!" shouted the driver. "You're blocking the road!"
"Just who do you think you are?" someone yelled.
The man pointed to the sign on his truck.
"You can read for yourself, maybe?"
The people gasped. "It's Izzy Pippik!"
"He's come at last!" cried Shaina.

She scooped up Yevka and raced to the truck.

"I'm Shaina!" she panted, thrusting the startled bird into his hands.

"My precious hen!" Pippik cried. "You found her!"

"I kept her for you," Shaina declared. "And the others, too."

Izzy Pippik scratched his beard.

"What others?"

Shaina pointed to the enormous flock fluttering about the square.

"But I only lost this hen," he said.

"These are her chicks, her chicks' chicks and her chicks' chicks' chicks,"
she explained. "If she's yours, they're all yours."

The hen struggled in Izzy Pippik's arms.

"Yevka, you must go with him," Shaina whispered.

The crowd began to howl.

"Please don't take our chickens! They've brought us such good fortune!"

Izzy Pippik looked at the anxious people and the contented flock. He peered into Shaina's unshakable eyes.

"All these birds are really mine?" he asked.

"Yes, Mr. Pippik." Shaina beamed.

He lovingly stroked Yevka's feathers.

Suddenly he tossed the hen out the truck window.

"What are you doing, Mr. Pippik?" Shaina gasped.

"I'm giving Yevka to you and her flock to the town."

"But you can't!"

"If they're mine to have," he chuckled, "they're mine to give."

Then Izzy Pippik blasted his horn.

AoooGAH!

With a warm-hearted wave, he puttered off through the cheering crowd.

Shaina burst into tears. Grandpa rushed over, and she buried her face in his coat.

"You were right, Shaina," he murmured. "Izzy Pippik did come."

"But he didn't take his chickens," she sobbed.

"Yes!" he exclaimed. "Isn't it wonderful?"

Shaina was shocked. "But they're his!"

"Are they, Shainala? Listen."

Shaina closed her eyes.

Roosters crowed. Children cheered. Hens cackled with glee.

"Happy days are here again!" the crowd merrily cried.

Suddenly Shaina felt a pickety peck on her toe, and her eyes popped open. She gazed thoughtfully at her feathered friend as the merriment chimed in her ears.

Suddenly she burst out laughing.

"Everyone knows it but me! You belong right here!"

BEEYAWWK!

The hen fluttered into her arms.

"Welcome home, Yevka," she cooed.

Bawwwk.

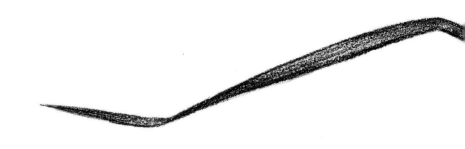

Better a hen tomorrow than an egg today — Chinese fortune cookie
Better an egg today than a hen tomorrow — Turkish proverb
For Mackenzie and Allora — A. D.

To Blima and Leopold Liebman, their son Sam and grandson Maximilien Lafrance Liebman — M. L.

Text © 2012 Aubrey Davis
Illustrations © 2012 Marie Lafrance

Kids Can Press acknowledges the financial support of the Government of Ontario, through the Ontario Media Development Corporation's Ontario Book Initiative; the Ontario Arts Council; the Canada Council for the Arts; and the Government of Canada, through the BPIDP, for our publishing activity.

Published in Canada by
Kids Can Press Ltd.
25 Dockside Drive
Toronto, ON M5A 0B5

Published in the U.S. by
Kids Can Press Ltd.
2250 Military Road
Tonawanda, NY 14150

www.kidscanpress.com

The artwork in this book was rendered in pencil and colored in Photoshop. The text is set in Garamond Premier Pro.

Edited by Debbie Rogosin and Sheila Barry
Designed by Marie Bartholomew

This book is smyth sewn casebound.
Manufactured in Tseung Kwan O, NT Hong Kong, China, in 10/2011 by Paramount Printing Co. Ltd.

CM 12 0 9 8 7 6 5 4 3 2 1

Library and Archives Canada Cataloguing in Publication

Davis, Aubrey
    A hen for Izzy Pippik / written by Aubrey Davis ; illustrated by Marie Lafrance.

ISBN 978-1-55453-243-8

I. Lafrance, Marie II. Title.

PS8557.A832H46 2012   jC813'.54   C2011-904728-4

Kids Can Press is a *corus*™ Entertainment company